P9-CMS-643

Eugene S Pattone

Sabina at School and the Letter S

Alphabet Friends

by Cynthia Klingel and Robert B. Noyed

The Child's World®

Published in the United States of America
by The Child's World®
P.O. Box 326
Chanhassen, MN 55317-0326
800-599-READ
www.childsworld.com

The Child's World®: Mary Berendes, Publishing Director

Editorial Directions, Inc.: E. Russell Primm, Editorial
Director; Emily Dolbear, Line Editor; Ruth Martin,
Editorial Assistant; Linda S. Koutris, Photo Researcher
and Selector

Photographs ©: Photomondo/Photodisc/Getty Images:
Cover& 9; O'Brien Productions/Corbis: 10; Corbis: 13;
Ariel Skelley/Corbis: 14; Ian Cartwirght/Photodisc/
Getty Images: 17; S. Meltzer/PhotoLink/Photodisc/
Getty Images: 18; F64/Photodisc/Getty Images: 21.

Library of Congress Cataloging-in-Publication Data
Klingel, Cynthia Fitterer.
  Sabina at school and the letter S / by Cynthia Klingel
and Robert B. Noyed.
    p. cm. — (Alphabet readers)
Summary: A simple story about a girl named Sabina's
first day in kindergarten introduces the letter "s".
  ISBN 1-59296-109-6 (Library Bound : alk. paper)
  [1. First day of school—Fiction. 2. Kindergarten—Fiction.
3. Alphabet.] I. Noyed, Robert B., ill. II. Title. III. Series.
  PZ7.K6798Sab 2003
  [E]—dc21   2003006607

Note to parents and educators:
The first skill children acquire before becoming successful readers is individual letter recognition. The Alphabet Friends series has been created with the needs of young learners in mind. Each engaging book begins by showing the difference between the capital letter and the lowercase letter. In each of the books on the vowels and the consonants c and g, children are introduced to the different sounds that the letter can make. Finally, children see that the letters can be found at the beginning of a word, in the middle of a word, and in most cases, at the end of a word.

Following the introduction, children meet their Alphabet Friends. The friend in each story encounters many words that include the featured letter of that book. Each noun that begins with the title letter is highlighted in red with the initial letter of the word in bold. Above the word is a rebus drawing that establishes a strong picture cue.

At the end of each book, we have included three words lists. Can your young learners find all the words in each book with the title letter in them?

Let's learn about the letter **S.**

The letter **S** can look like this: **S.**

The letter **S** can also look like this: **s.**

The letter **s** can be at the beginning of a word, like starfish.

starfish

The letter **s** can be in the middle of a word, like newspaper.

new**s**paper

The letter **s** can be at the
end of a word, like grass.

gras**s**

Sabina is feeling a little shy. It is her first

day of school. Sabina is six years old.

Ms. Suarez is Sabina's kindergarten

teacher.

Sabina takes the bus to **s**chool. She sits

with her friends on the bus. They are

all excited for the first day of **s**chool.

Sabina meets Ms. Suarez at school.

Ms. Suarez welcomes her students to

the first day. She shows the students

where to sit.

Ms. Suarez and the students do many

things during the first day. They sing

songs. Some songs are silly!

Ms. Suarez reads a **s**tory. It tells about

a **s**tarfish that lives in the **s**ea. The **s**tudents

like the **s**tory. They learn about life in

the **s**ea.

The **s**tudents do art projects. Everyone

makes a colorful **s**tarfish. They use their

scissors to cut the paper. **S**abina hangs

her **s**tarfish in the **s**chool hallway.

Sabina is a little sad. The day is done!

She has had a super day. Sabina thinks

of another day at school and smiles.

Fun Facts

A **sea** is a body of salt water. Sometimes the word **sea** is used to refer to the ocean—the body of salt water that covers most of Earth's surface. Sometimes the word **sea** refers to a smaller body of water that is part of the ocean, but also partly surrounded by land. The Caribbean **S**ea, for example, is right off the Atlantic Ocean. It is enclosed by South America to the south and Central America to the west, and partially surrounded by islands to the north and east.

A **s**tarfish, also called a sea star, is not really a fish. A **s**tarfish is a sea animal with five or more arms. When a **s**tarfish has five arms, it looks like a star. But some species of **s**tarfish have as many as 40 arms. Many types of **s**tarfish can regenerate, or regrow, new arms. That means if you cut a **s**tarfish in two, each piece could become a new animal!

To Read More

About the Letter S

Flanagan, Alice K. *Sam: The Sound of S.* Chanhassen, Minn.: The Child's World,
   2000.

About the Sea

MacDonald, Suse. *Sea Shapes.* San Diego: Harcourt Brace, 1994.

Reasoner, Charles. *Who's in the Sea?.* Los Angeles: Price Stern Sloan, 1995.

Serafini, Kristin Joy Pratt. *A Swim through the Sea.* Nevada City, Calif.: Dawn
   Publications, 1994.

About Starfish

Fowler, Allen. *Stars of the Sea.* Danbury, Conn.: Children's Press, 2000.

Ridinger, Gayle, and Andreina Parpajola (illustrator). *At the Bottom of the Sea.*
   Milwaukee: Gareth Stevens, 2002.

Words with S

Words with S at the Beginning

Sabina
Sabina's
sad
school
scissors
sea
she
shows
shy
silly
sing
sit
sits
six
smiles
some
songs
starfish
story
students
Suarez
super

Words with S in the Middle

also
first
grass
newspaper
scissors
starfish
use

Words with S at the End

bus
friends
grass
hangs
has
is
lives
makes
meets
Ms.
projects
reads
Sabina's
scissors
shows
sits
smiles
songs
students
takes
tells
things
this
welcomes
years

About the Authors

Cynthia Klingel has worked as a high school English teacher and an elementary teacher. She is currently the curriculum director for a Minnesota school district. Cynthia Klingel lives with her family in Mankato, Minnesota.

Robert B. Noyed started his career as a newspaper reporter. Since then, he has worked in communications and public relations for a Minnesota school district for more than fourteen years. Robert B. Noyed lives with his family in Brooklyn Center, Minnesota.